Little Robin follows this story very closely. Can you find him in every scene?

CHRISTMAS HUGS FOR TANJA, MONIKA AND LUKA

HODDER CHILDREN'S BOOKS

First published in Great Britain in 2017
by Hodder and Stoughton

Text and illustrations copyright © David Melling, 2017

The moral rights of the author have been asserted.

A CIP catalogue record for this book
is available from the British Library.

PB ISBN: 978 1 444 94236 1
HB ISBN: 978 1 444 90683 7

10 9 8 7 6 5 4 3 2 1

Printed and bound in China

Hodder Children's Books
An imprint of Hachette Children's Group
Part of Hodder and Stoughton
Carmelite House
50 Victoria Embankment
London EC4Y 0DZ

An Hachette UK Company

www.hachette.co.uk
www.hachettechildrens.co.uk

MERRY CHRISTMAS, HUGLESS DOUGLAS

David Melling

Hodder
Children's
Books

'It's Christmas Eve at last!'
cried Douglas and he ran through the snow
as fast as he could. He wanted to make the
most of every single minute.

Douglas was so full of hugs he gave some
to the trees. But no matter how many
he hugged, he still had more to give.

'DOES ANYONE WANT A CHRISTMAS HUG?'
Douglas called.
He listened to his echo bounce off the trees.

Then - POOMFF! -

a snowball!

'Merry Christmas, Douglas!' laughed his friends. And before Douglas could say anything

– POOMFF! POOMFF! POOMFF! –

snowballs came flying in from all sides!

'Haha, I look like a snowman,' said Douglas.
'If we hung decorations on you, you'd look like
a snowy Christmas tree!' said Little Sheep.

'Oooh, what shall we do,' said
the Funny Bunnies, 'build a
snowman or decorate Douglas?'

'Snowman first!' said Douglas.

He began scooping handfuls of snow and rolling them into a giant snowball. But the more he rolled, the more his friends disappeared.

'There, finished!' panted Douglas, and he gave his new friend a SNOWMAN HUG.

'Thank you!' said the Snowman.

'You can talk!'

'Yes, we can!' cried his friends.

Douglas yelped and nearly fell over.

Everyone stopped laughing when
they heard a funny jingle noise.

Jingle
Jingle
Help!

'I think it's coming from those trees,'
said Little Sheep.

So they set off to see what they could find.

At the top of the hill, there was a little upside-down reindeer hanging from a fallen tree. He had a very shiny nose that jingled when he smiled.

His name was Rudi
and he had a story to tell
about flying, getting
lost in the woods and
Christmas magic.

Little Sheep still wanted to decorate something
and pointed at the fallen tree.

'But it's too big to get home,' Douglas sighed.

Rudi's nose jingled and glowed a little brighter.
'I can help with that. Let's fly down!'

'Are you sure about this?' said Douglas.

'WHEEEE!' cried Rudi.

'It's a Christmas miracle!' yelped Little Sheep.

PLUMPFFF!

'Oh,' said Douglas, 'the tree's a bit broken.'

Rudi's nose jingled again.

'With a bit of Christmas magic,' he said,
'we can make our own tree.'

So they did, and this is what it looked like... until...

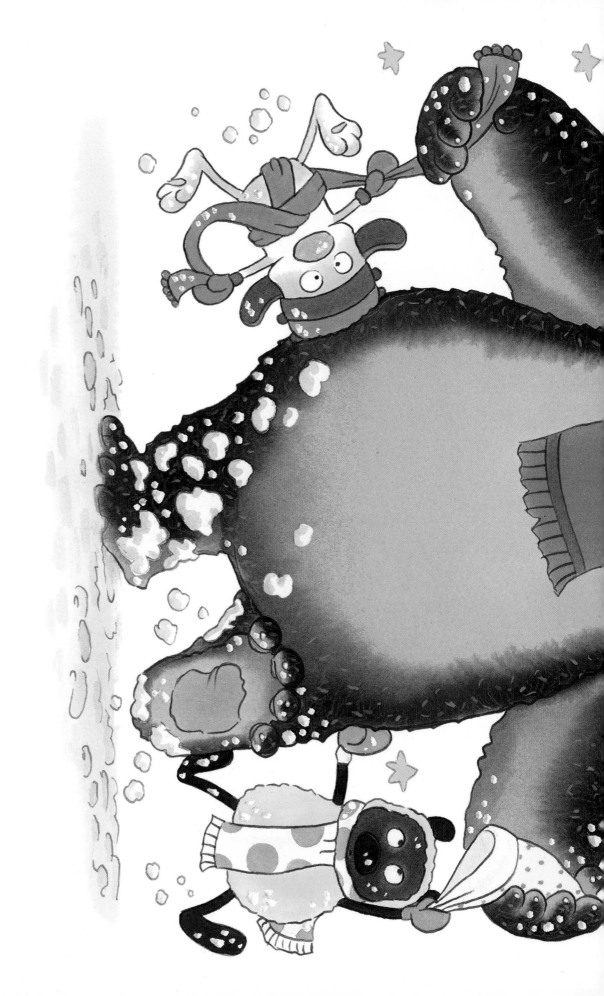

…they all fell down and made snow angels instead!

Then the first twinkle of stars reminded Rudi he should be on his way to help a very special person.

'Will we see you again?' asked Douglas, sadly.

'Of course,' said Rudi. 'I'll wave as I fly by, tonight and every Christmas.'

So when Douglas and his friends got home,
just before bed, they shared a hug and
searched the sky for Rudi.

'MERRY CHRISTMAS, RUDI!' called Douglas.
'MERRY CHRISTMAS, EVERYONE!'

THINGS TO DO AT CHRISTMAS TIME...

Pull Christmas crackers

Cut paper angels

Write a letter to Santa

Kiss under mistletoe

Hug presents

Look out for new
magical friends

Build a snowman

Ring bells

Sing carols

Decorate the tree

ADVENT HUG JAR

Why not make an ADVENT HUG JAR?

A collecting jar of your **favourite** hugs for you to choose,
one for each day of December, right up to **Christmas!**

YOU WILL NEED...

A jar or pot

Stickers, ribbon or glitter

24 slips of paper

1. Decorate your jar to look lovely and **Christmassy**

2. Write a **different type of hug** on each slip of paper then put them in the jar

3. Each day of December, read one of the pieces of paper and have a **hug-filled** Christmas

Here are some examples of
HUGS you can do:

JINGLE BELL HUG

CHRISTMAS TREE HUG

PRESENT HUG

SNOW HUG

REINDEER HUG